For Chris, Clio, and Isla—who make everything fun.
—D.P.

For Eli, because you're you.
—M.B.

Text copyright © 2015 by Dev Petty
Cover art and interior illustrations copyright © 2015 by Mike Boldt

Dragonfly Books with the colophon is a registered trademark of Penguin Random House LLC.

Visit us on the Web! rhcbooks.com

Educators and librarians, for a variety of teaching tools, visit us at RHTeachersLibrarians.com

The Library of Congress has cataloged the hardcover edition of this work as follows:
Petty, Dev.
I don't want to be a frog / by Dev Petty ; illustrated by Mike Boldt. — First edition.
pages cm.
Summary: A frog who yearns to be any animal that is cute and warm discovers that being wet,
slimy, and full of bugs has its advantages.
ISBN 978-0-385-37866-6 (trade) — ISBN 978-0-375-97334-5 (lib. bdg.) —
ISBN 978-0-375-98234-7 (ebook)
[1. Self-acceptance—Fiction. 2. Frogs—Fiction. 3. Animals—Fiction.] I. Boldt, Mike, illustrator.
II. Title. III. Title: I do not want to be a frog.
PZ7.P448138Iaaf 2015 [E]—dc23 2014012949

ISBN 978-1-9848-5208-3 (pbk.)

MANUFACTURED IN CHINA
10 9 8
First Dragonfly Books Edition

I DON'T WANT TO BE A FROG

written by Dev Petty

illustrated by Mike Boldt

DRAGONFLY BOOKS • NEW YORK

I don't like being a Frog. It's too **Slimy**.

That may be. But you can't be a Rabbit.

I want to be a **Pig.**